Frank
and the
Big Mistake

Martha Brockenbrough

illustrated by Jon Lau

LEVINE QUERIDO

MONTCLAIR · AMSTERDAM · HOBOKEN

This is an Arthur A. Levine book
Published by Levine Querido

LEVINE QUERIDO

www.levinequerido.com • info@levinequerido.com
Levine Querido is distributed by Chronicle Books, LLC
Text copyright © 2024 by Martha Brockenbrough
Illustrations copyright © 2024 by Jon Lau
All rights reserved
Library of Congress Control Number: 2023951396
Hardcover ISBN 978-1-64614-460-0
Paperback ISBN 978-1-64614-499-0
Printed and bound in China

Published in November 2024
First Printing
The text type was set in Baskerville Regular
Jon Lau created the illustrations for
this picture book by painting the characters, objects,
and backgrounds using poster color paints on sheets
of BFK Rives printmaking paper.
He then scanned the paintings and assembled the illustrations
in Adobe Photoshop, much like a digital collage.

For Jolie and Ann. —M.B.

For Sam, Nikko, Junyi, Aimee, Szu, Mon-Lai, Tory, Elle, Lynn, Emily, and Panini. —J.L.

CHAPTER 1

What's a Nibling?

Cap'n Keith would not stop squawking.

"Nibling," he said. "Nibling!"

"Shh," Frank said. "Sunny is asleep in a sunbeam."

"NIBLING!" Cap'n Keith used his loudest squawk. He flapped his wings.

Frank knew Cap'n Keith was trying to tell him something important. But now was not the time.

"NIBLING!"

Sunny grunted. She stretched and yawned. Frank loved her pink tongue.

"Fraaaaaank," Sunny whined, "Teach Cap'n Keith the rules of naps. You do not wake someone up from a nap."

"Rules of naps," Cap'n Keith said. "Ha. As if."

Then he squawked again. "Nibling! Nibling."

"Frank," Sunny said, "What is a nibling?"

Frank knew the answer. It was like the word "nibble."

It is what you do if you are not terribly hungry or if the Whiskies in your bowl are stale.

"A nibling is a small bite of a thing," Frank said. "Like a taste."

He walked into the kitchen. Sunny followed.

"Oooooh," Sunny said. "Niblings sound yummy."

"They can be," Frank said. "They can also be dry and bland."

"Sticks are dry and bland," Sunny said. "But I still love them."

Frank sniffed his Whiskies. Fresh enough. He nibbled.

Sunny slurped her water. Sunny could not have food out all the time.

She did not have Frank's self-control.

Then the doorbell rang.

"NIBLING!" Cap'n Keith squawked.

Frank and Sunny's humans opened the door.

"NIBLING!"

They raced to the door.

"Time for a taste," Sunny said.

CHAPTER 2

Nobody Wants to Be Tasted

The Nibling stood in the doorway. The Nibling did not look delicious.

Sunny did not care. She zoomed in fast circles on the rug.

This was her welcome dance.

The humans yelled, "Sunny! Sunny!"

Frank knew that they wanted Sunny to be still.

But Sunny did not know this.

Sunny thought they liked her welcome dance and wanted more fast circles.

Sunny made circles until she could not walk straight.

She wobbled to the child.

"Time to taste!" she said.

The grown-up humans did not understand Sunny the way Frank understood Sunny.

But the Nibling understood. The Nibling shrieked.

"Oh, no," Frank thought.

"A nibling isn't a small taste of something. It is a small person who is a family member."

Frank knew this now. He also knew he'd taught Sunny a wrong thing. He had made a big mistake.

"Sunny," he said.

But he was too late. There were Sunny's teeth. There was her pink tongue.

"Snap!"

And there was her leash. One of the humans hooked Sunny up and jerked her away before she tasted the Nibling.

"Bad girl, Sunny. Bad girl."

Sunny cried.

Sunny did not know what she had done wrong. Frank knew. Nobody wanted to be tasted.

Sunny was locked in her crate.

This was Frank's fault.

Then his human said, "Frank, this is Nellie, our Nibling."

And his other human said, "Nellie, this is Frank."

Nellie clapped her small hands.

"Make good choices," the human said.

"Uh-oh," Cap'n Keith squawked.

"Kitty," Nellie said. "Kitty."

Nellie lifted Frank.

She put him in a basket.

Frank puffed up his handsome fur. He bent his ears back.

Nobody puts Frank in a basket.

CHAPTER 3

Frank in the Guest Room

Nellie carried Frank around the house in the basket.

Frank felt seasick.

"Scan the horizon," Cap'n Keith said. "The horizon helps."

But the horizon was outside. Frank could not see outside.

He could see basket. He could see Nellie's small hand. That small hand was stronger than it looked. That small hand could really swing a basket.

"Whee!" Nellie said. "Whee!"

"Meow," Frank said. "Hiss."

He wished for his keyboard.

He would type a strongly worded letter.

The letter would have read, "I do not care to ride in baskets. A basket is an okay place for a nap, but only if you have chosen to sleep there. That is called consent."

He could not write a letter, though. He could go along with the ride. He could try not to yarf. That was all. Finally, Nellie's small, strong hand got tired. She set down the basket.

Franked peeked out. They were in the guest room. Frank and Sunny were not allowed in the guest room. The humans kept their collections there. Dolls and knickknacks, mostly.

"And we need one place in this

house that has no fur," they always said.

That made Frank mad. Frank took baths every day with his own rough tongue.

Frank used his rough tongue to scrape off fur. He used his wet mouth to roll fur into neat balls. He used his strong throat to cough up these damp balls.

Nobody else was that tidy.

Nellie lifted Frank out of the basket. She put him on the bed. It was nice and soft.

"Maybe this won't be too bad," Frank thought.

Far away, Sunny whined. Oh dear. Frank could not stay in the soft bed. He had to save his friend. He leapt.

But his feet did not touch the floor. Nellie's fast hands grabbed him first. She held him close.

"Not the basket," he thought. "Anything but that."

Nellie did not put him in the basket.

She put him in something much, much worse.

CHAPTER 4

Pretty Kitty

"Be still, kitty," Nellie said.

It was hard to be still, when small, strong hands are putting your legs into clown pants.

Clown pants do not have a hole for a tail. Frank did not like to have his tail tucked into pants. It felt weird. It felt bunchy.

But it felt worse when small hands put you in a clown smock with a ruffled neck.

Frank did not need a clown smock or clown pants. He did not need a ruffled neck.

He was born in a tuxedo. That is the best kind of suit. That is why his humans wore them to fancy parties. There is no better way to hide your skin.

"Pretty kitty," Nellie said.

Frank did not know what to say.

He knew he was pretty. But he was not pretty because he had on clown pants and a clown smock with a ruffled neck.

He was pretty because he was Frank.

Nellie filled the basket with dolls.

That was a relief, Frank thought. No more basket.

Nellie lifted Frank. She draped him over her shoulder. She lifted the basket.

Frank could not see where they were walking. He could only see where they had been.

Even so, he knew where he was.

That's because Cap'n Keith said, "Frank! Ha! Look at you!"

And Sunny said, "Help me, Frank. You are my only hope."

Frank's heart sank. If your only hope is a cat in a clown suit, you are in trouble.

Nellie put the dolls in chairs.

"Time for the wedding," she said.

"A wedding," Frank thought. "I wonder who is getting married."

Frank liked weddings. He planned to marry the magnificent, masked cat that sometimes ate apple cores from the trash. He had written many love letters for her to eat instead.

"Pretty bird," Nellie said.

"I know," Cap'n Keith said.

Nellie opened his cage. She pulled him out.

"Yikes!" Cap'n Keith said. "What's up?"

"A wedding," Nellie said, "for you and kitty."

CHAPTER 5

The Quickie Wedding

Frank looked at Cap'n Keith.

Cap'n Keith looked at Frank.

They both squawked.

"Stand here," Nellie said.

She set Frank on the rug. She set Cap'n Keith next to Frank. Cap'n Keith smelled like chicken. Frank liked chicken.

"Help me, Sunny," Frank said.

"I can't, Frank," Sunny said. "I am locked up. I am a criminal."

"On the count of three," Nellie said, "You be married."

"Frank, are you getting married?" Sunny said. "Let me out! I want to watch!"

"One," Nellie said.

"No," Frank said. "This cannot be real."

For once, Cap'n Keith did not say a thing. His beak clacked. His feathers shook.

"Two," Nellie said.

"It sounds as if you will be married in one second," Sunny said.

One second is not much time.

But this second felt like forever to Frank.

He could feel his tail, bunched up in the clown pants. He could feel the ruffled clown collar brush his whiskers.

And he could feel something happen to his heart. If his heart had been a mouth, it would have screamed. Or yarfed.

Instead, it made Frank go berserk.

Frank zoomed across the rug. He turned a corner so fast his feet zipped up the wall. He crashed into Cap'n Keith's cage and knocked it down.

Frank felt like he could run up the chimney and launch himself into space. He could be the first cat on Mars.

"Frank has the zoomies," Sunny said. "I did not think he had it in him."

Then the humans arrived.

"What's going on here?" one asked.

"Why are the dolls in chairs?" the other asked. "Why is Cap'n Keith out of his cage?"

"And why is Frank in clown pants?"

"For the wedding," Nellie said.

Frank zoomed.

CHAPTER 6

Good News and Bad News

Frank zoomed all the way under the bed.

The good news: The clown pants came off.

The bad news: The clown smock did not.

"This smock is nibbling my face," Frank thought.

It is hard to breathe under a bed when a clown smock is nibbling your face.

But things could have been worse.

Frank could have been on his honeymoon.

A honeymoon is a trip you take after a wedding. He did not want to take that trip with Cap'n Keith.

He just wanted to be friends. "Frank, there you are." One of the humans peered under the bed.

"Wow," the other human said.

Wow was a small word that said a lot, Frank knew.

He also knew that this was not a good wow, like the wow you say when someone has poured a fresh bowl of Whiskies.

This was a wow that you said when you did not want your mouth to laugh.

"Please do not laugh," Frank thought.

Frank's humans did

not laugh. One used gentle hands to slide Frank out from under the bed. The other slid Frank out of the clown smock.

"Much better," the humans said.

It was better. But it was far from good.

Sunny was still in jail. Cap'n Keith had not squawked. He might be dead. He was no spring chicken.

"There will not be a wedding," the human said. "We have informed Nellie."

"But what about Sunny?" Frank asked.

His human pretended that he could not understand what Frank said.

He scratched Frank on the chin, the way Frank liked.

Frank purred and braced himself for the worst.

CHAPTER 7

A Wedding Toast

But the worst did not happen.

The human carried Frank to the kitchen.

Everyone was in there. Cap'n Keith was in his cage. Sunny was out of her crate. Frank's other human and Nellie were in chairs.

"I am out of jail, Frank," Sunny said. "It was a misunderstanding."

"Puppies get excited," a human told Nellie. "Sunny did not want to eat you."

"Niblings get excited," the other human told Frank. "You are still a single cat."

"The puppy is nice," Nellie said. "Her fur is soft. She smells like grass. Her tongue is medium pink. That is the best pink. I do not even mind her hot breath."

Frank looked at Nellie.

The Nibling had put him in a basket. She had tried to make him marry a bird he did not love instead of the masked cat he did.

Those were bad things.

But the Nibling liked Sunny.

That was a good thing. It was the best thing.

"We are sorry we called off the wedding," one human said.

"But we can still make wedding toasts," the other human said.

"I like toasts," Nellie said. "Especially with butter and jam."

"Avocado spread is better for you," the other human said.

"Gross," Nellie said.

Frank did not think anything could taste worse than stale Whiskies.

He was wrong. Plain toast was worse. But he was getting used to being wrong.

Cap'n Keith liked his toast.

"More cracker!" he squawked. "More cracker."

"Toast is dry and has no taste," Sunny said. "It is like a stick. I love toast!"

"I am glad," Frank said.

And he was. Maybe not about the toast.

He was glad he could be in this warm kitchen.

He liked how the humans ate their toast and avocado spread.

He liked how the Nibling had hers with jam.

He liked it when Sunny was not in her crate.

He liked it when Cap'n Keith was in his cage where he could be safe.

He even liked Sunny's hot breath and Cap'n Keith's loud squawks. That is how Frank knew his friends were okay.

And Frank? He was okay, too, even though he had worn clown pants and a smock and almost had a wedding.

The humans held up their toasts. "To family—the family we have made," they said.

Frank purred. That's what family was, he thought. Family loved you, even when you made a big mistake.

Frank looked at the Nibling. Did she still love him?

The Nibling finished her toast. She clapped her small hands.

She scratched Frank's chin the just way he liked.

So Frank leaned in. He leaned in and he purred.